UGLY
GUIDE
TO EATING OUT
AND KEEPING IT DOWN

TO ALITA, DREW, JIM, GERRY, ALEX, NICOLE, KATE, CATHY, JASON, SUSAN, AND BABO

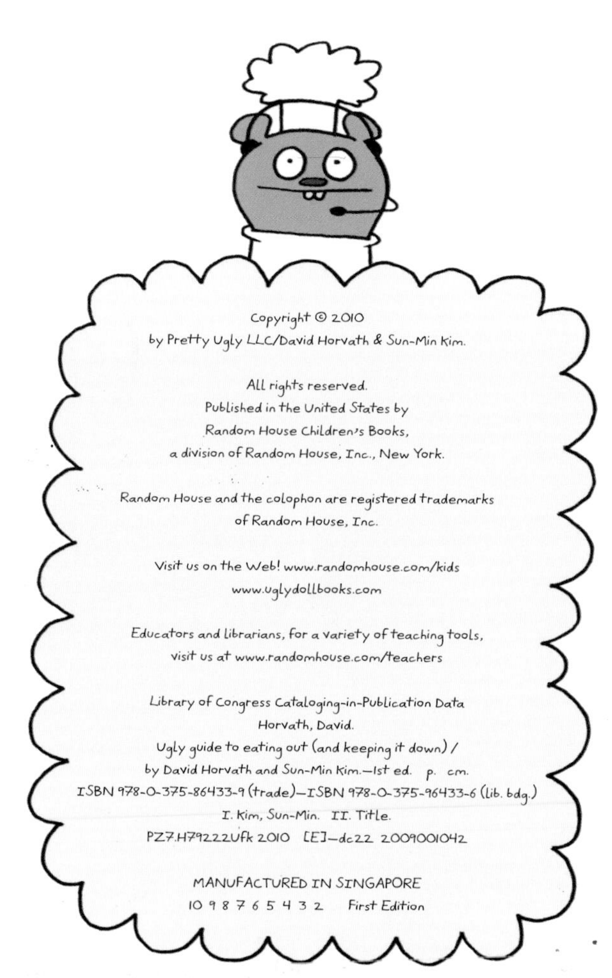

Published in the United States by
Random House Children's Books,
a division of Random House, Inc., New York.

Random House and the colophon are registered trademarks
of Random House, Inc.

Visit us on the Web! www.randomhouse.com/kids
www.uglydollbooks.com

Educators and librarians, for a variety of teaching tools,
visit us at www.randomhouse.com/teachers

Library of Congress Cataloging-in-Publication Data
Horvath, David.
Ugly guide to eating out (and keeping it down) /
by David Horvath and Sun-Min Kim.—1st ed. p. cm.
ISBN 978-0-375-86433-9 (trade)—ISBN 978-0-375-96433-6 (lib. bdg.)
I. Kim, Sun-Min. II. Title.
PZ7.H79222Ufk 2010 [E]—dc22 2009001042

MANUFACTURED IN SINGAPORE
10 9 8 7 6 5 4 3 2 First Edition

UGLY GUIDE

TO EATING OUT AND KEEPING IT DOWN

by David Horvath & Sun-Min Kim

RANDOM HOUSE NEW YORK

TRUNKO

WINKOLINA

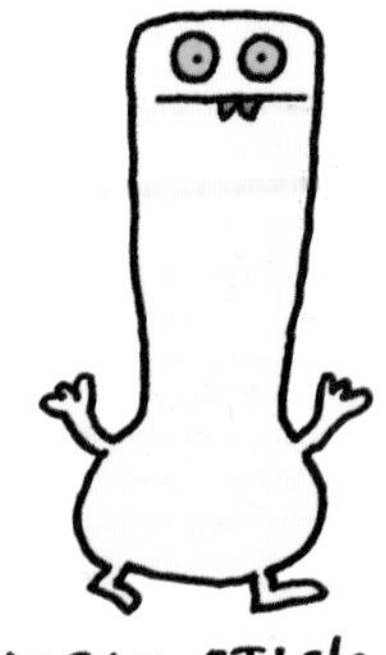
UGLY STICK

UPPY

UGLYDOG

JEERO

wedgehead

BABO

wage

BIG TOE

PLUNKO

PUGLEE

MR. KASOOGI
TRAY
ICE-BAT
BABO'S BIRD

MRS. KASOOGI

TURNY BERNIE

MOXY

OX

KAIJU ICE-BAT

POE

UGLY GHOST

UGLYWORM

Nothing BEATS A HOME-COOKED MEAL

Eat up! If you're hungry and in need of nourishment, nothing beats a home-cooked meal—especially one that's cooked in your own home! Watch out for those meals cooked at somebody else's house, though!

Remember that holding your nose while eating or yelling "Yuck!" and spitting it out might just be considered rude. Check first.

CALL FOR DELIVERY

When the Uglys don't feel like cooking (or don't know how), they call upon the greatest invention since food-delivery uniforms . . . food delivery! In Uglytown, there are many different types of cuisine to choose from: oily, greasy, messy, or go-for-the-mystery-bucket!

Just keep in mind that ordering in on a daily basis can give rise to harmful side effects, such as having no money left to tip the delivery guy, which can, in turn, lead to the delivery guy's macho cousin coming over to personally feed you . . . his fist!

Running behind? Late for school? Well, you should have left earlier, because the line at the Ugly Drive-Thru is always LONG! Somebody please tell Wedgehead it's the same menu on both sides! The drive-thru guys are equipped with boy-band headsets to help you get the food you need and the songs you could do without.

You may not realize it, but all drive-thru speakers are actually karaoke machines! Next time you pull up, sing a few bars and watch the magic unfold! (The police in the Uglyverse possess magical powers.)

Oh, and if you are delivering pizza, please don't drive through the competition's drive-thru in the company car. That's just bad form. And the tabloids will be all over it.

SUPERMARKET TASTE-TEST-O-RAMA

Uglytown is Free-Sample City! You just have to know where to look. Watch out, though: the Smarty Supermarket managers are getting hip to the free-sample tag teams, so act natural. Eat casual. Try to look like you're not enjoying it. You know, like when Mom cooks.

Trunko and Babo make a great taste-test tag team. The idea is to share! Well, that was the idea, anyway.

The Ugly Mall hosts many a corporate taste test, so you can pretty much chow down all day long. Just remain undecided and keep saying, "Wait, lemme try that one again." Until the taste-tester guy starts to look at you funny. Then come back with sunglasses on and say, "Yeah, I'm not that other guy who was just here." Okay, no. Don't do that.

FAST FOOD!

"Hey, not so fast!" That's the catchy jingle refrain of Tako Hut, and all Uglys grow up singing it.

Don't worry if the place looks empty. That just means MORE FOR YOU!

Oh, and if you feel dizzy or strange after eating a few of their famous Tako Cones, their spongy Tako Shake will absorb all that acid in no time.

GET them to get MORE
SPICY Long things
TAKO TACO Burger
TAKO JUICE
A SMILE IS OUR GOAL... WE'LL SETTLE FOR NO FROWN.
ARE you sure IT'S ok to eat this?
Tako Hut has the best work environment. With only one or two customers coming in a day, there's practically no mess to clean up! So some employees just skip the cleaning part altogether!
I'll try something HEALTHY.
what do you mean?
For faster, friendlier service, minimize the back talk to the drive-thru window guy. (At participating locations.)
The WAITER'S TAKing Forever.
There IS one?

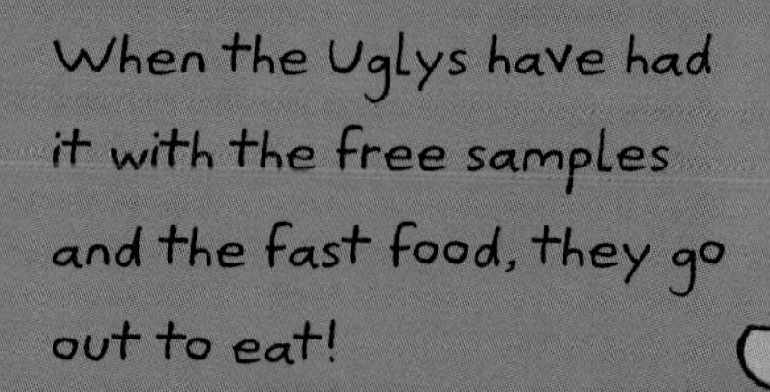

When the Uglys have had it with the free samples and the fast food, they go out to eat!

NOW OPEN
CAFE POE
SUPER-HOT STUFF
ICE-BAT
URA CONCOU
OK By me
URAコンコー
UG-L
EAT
yes
OK
DON'T YOU DO IT!
MINA WAS HERE 611
スーパー OK
U CAN WALK
611

EAT iT UP UPTOWN

If you have the money or win the lottery, make a reservation at Chez Fancy Pants!

Prices are higher than the moon and portions smaller than a pea! Fine dining at its best, Chez Fancy Pants is the most expensive restaurant in the Uglyverse! Chez Fancy Pants has seating by the window so the Uglys inside can show off the amount of money they no longer have! Wait, that doesn't sound right.

WHICH FORK IS FOR BERRY PIE?

I just eat here to show off to other show-offs. The only folks who would be at all impressed aren't eating here.

Chez Fancy Pants is located uptown, around the corner from Ox and Wedgehead's Coatcheck-2-Go cart. Technically speaking, the coatcheck is inside the restaurant, so deal with Ox and Wedgehead at your own risk. Especially when it's cold outside!

Once you've finished the meal, they bring the check in a very lovely leather-case thingy . . . and no worries, the carpet is extra fluffy, in case you keel over backward in shock when you see the size of the bill.

I FOUND the FANCY PART!

the check $

BROWN-BAG iT!
MAKES A great puppet when you're Done!
I found this in the OFFICE FRIDGE!
Hey, my MOLD EXPERIMENT!
WINKOLINA
Nothing makes for a more exciting lunch than letting it sit around in a brown paper bag. Just be sure to write your name on it if you leave it in the fridge, unless, that is, you are known for having good lunches. In that case, make up a name.
I'm the KID who always has a wet paper Bag.
I'll eat IT!
Ever notice that some kids always seem to have that odd wet spot on their brown paper bag and all that fruit flying out?
MAYBE MEAL
BLIND BAG LUNCH
Stay Back!
GOSH, I hope IT'S LUNCH AND NOT A SPRING SNAKE!
OX'S
LUCKY-DRAW
MAYBE MEAL
DELi

It's been fun swapping lunch, but are you ready for Ox and Wedgehead's Lucky-Draw Deli Bags? You could wind up getting the best lunch ever! Or the worst lunch ever! Or maybe no lunch at all. The only thing they don't have is a free lunch.

The best brown-bag lunch brings on instant popularity. It also means going hungry, because it's the giving-away part that makes you so popular. The trick is to bring egg salad every day.

ACTION
HERO
what dat
he's one too
WEDGEHEAD
FROZEN MELTED ICE
yo ho
UH-OH
This water is wet! Send it Back!
EATS your LUNCH For you!
BIG TONY'S
SHRUNKEN LAMB
I need A Jacket!
LUNCH with texture!
I Don't see IT
?

32-BiT
LUNCH-
UPGRADE ADD-ON
X
8MEG MODE
XYZ
DUUUUU UUUDE!
8 MEGS!
UPGRADE your FOOD
ALTERNATE DIMENSION
LUNCHAMUNCH
ALTernate Lunch Time!
MOSTLY
OK TASTE
OFF-the-RADAR LUNCH
Cheese 'N' IMITATION CAR TIRE!
Don't eat 'N' swim!
Deep Doo Doo
UFO MEAL
ALIEN DISCLOSURE-o-meter
OPENS when the FILES OPEN!
Come On!
TIME-Release LUNCH
SUPER HUNGRY!

FOOD FROM FARAWAY LANDS

In the Uglyverse, it's said that you haven't lived until you've tried all the different kinds of food in the world. But whoever said that never tried Ghosty Burgers! Ech! The Uglys do enjoy cuisine from lands afar, though. The best way to get to know a new land is to sample its food . . . go ahead, try it. You first.

Wage comes from a part of town where cookies are rare and not truly appreciated. He tries to keep a straight face when he's over at Babo's place for breakfast. All they seem to eat at his place are cookies. Wait. Wage always has a straight face. Well, he's probably smiling on the inside.

Trying foods from faraway lands and other cultures isn't enough for the Uglys. They like to try tastes from alternate dimensions and spirit realms as well . . . if there is such a thing. Ghosty Burgers have a smell you won't believe!

JEERO'S COZY PLACE ON THE CORNER
WELCOME to our quaint Little getaway... Oh, your whoLe Party hasn't arrived? Yeah, Sit Back down, PaL.
NEXT!
Jeero's Cozy Place on the Corner has lots of character and ambience. The smoke-filled kitchen gives off an early-morning-fog-like atmosphere, and the staff will make you dizzy with their flair. (That's Jeero in many quick costume changes.)
Today's special is yesterday's tough sell.
KID'S Burger!
NICE Move, that's always the cheapest.

The prices are okay if you're smart. The trick is to know your food. Sure, the Super Spicy Burger is cheap, but the tap water costs a fortune. Peanuts and salt chips are free! So BYOW. The tables at Jeero's are very close together, so you'll get to know your neighbors really well. You'll know they're talking about you if it suddenly gets quiet and their eyes move around funny. Unless they pay extra for Jeero's sign-card system. Then you're on your own. In the summer, Jeero opens up his famous Fire Pit Balcony Terrace! Take in the magnificent view, but cross your fingers!

Family restaurants are super-popular in Uglytown. You could wait eons to be seated!

Luckily, they pass around these electronic flashy things, just to be sure you don't wander too far while you're waiting for your table (or try finding a table at the place across the street).

GET READY! You're GONNA See STUFF Like...
the kitchen
TREASURE MAP PLACE MAT
OLD Bike
GRAB BAG
BEST UNIFORM EVER!
The check with TIP BAG
ROMANTIC FAKE CANDLE
FREE when you Buy
TRICKY COUPON
Huge ICED TEA with TINY straw and Restroom Tokens.
they're open!
HAPPY customers
Long wait!
Happy CAMPers
Peace out.
Happy to go home
AWESOME DECOR
OX
STOP
OLD SCHOOL
I KNOW OLD BIKES ON A WALL MAKE ME hungry!
Is that Decor or was there an accident?
GULP!
My garage sale has come Back to haunt me!
is this for REAL?

Watch out for these delicious delis on wheels!

You know what the ice cream truck song sounds like, but just wait till you hear the call of the Bug'n'Bun on a nice, quiet night. Very lifelike!

Here are the more popular carts to look for.

Uglys LOVE eating at Theme Restaurant! What's the theme? It changes all the time. Some nights it's movies and stars, and other nights it's rock 'n' roll. But whatever the theme, it's loud-colored leather jackets and pricey key chains every night of the week.

The Theme Restaurant gift shop is always open! They know how much you would hate to forget that $40 salad you just ate, so now there's no way you will ever do that.

HEALTH iNSPECTOR
CHECKLiST
WASH your hands OF IT.
ALL CLEAN
wash your hands well!
¢O¢
wash your BAD, BAD Score away!
NEW
STINKY
OLD MILK SUIT
High Hopes of No old cheese
why, what?
Come on, Less Bugs
Look-the-other-way specs
So DiRTY You need a Miracle to clean it
Book OF SPELLS
you should see the BIG one!
MOVE IT, SUCKA!
Health CODE VIOLATION REMOVER
"good thing you don't have a nose!"
Mystery FooD BAG
Please, NO old cheese TODAY.
Mr. BOSS MAN

WISH I were HERE!
Postcard to yourself
I Don't take BRIBes, But I Do take DonaTIONS For my new Suit and Tie FOUNDATION
That's going to Be Some SUIT!
I HATE OLD cheese!
Go ahead.
OK...
SAMPLES to Bring Back to LAB
ASSISTANT
Chef AWAY
CHEF SPRAY
you go First.
ooh Boy
The Restaurants of uglytown keep me very Busy.
CLEANUP CREW
cleanup after the cleanup crew...crew
...I mean, Like, Really Dirty Dishes.
Dude, no way.
wanna help me at work?
No way! are you NUTS?!
A sympathetic ear
ProFessional HeLP

WHO PAYS?

Here comes the tricky part!

Who should pick up the check?

Should you take turns?

Who goes first?

I got it THIS time!
Thank you, DADDY!
You can always tell when it's NOT Ox's turn to pay . . . he doesn't stop eating! Little does he know that Wedgehead is still broke from the last time they ate out. Time to wash some dishes! (Somebody has to!)
That uncomfortable moment...
It's Been ten Minutes!
we Don't have Arms.

When he can't get customers to eat at his Cozy Place on the Corner, Jeero cooks up a storm at his Sneak Attack Snack Shack, where the snacks sneak-attack your taste buds and your stomach never forgives you!

With its retro style and Jeero's use of such quaint phrases as "Golly gee" and "Holy smoke," Jeero's Sneak Attack Snack Shack will bring back that special feeling people had long before you were born. (Gulp.)

The booths shrink with each visit so you can all grow closer every time you stop by. Hmm, wait, is the booth really getting smaller? Uh-oh!

Big Toe Bistro was a war zone until Big Toe strung all-white holiday lights in the ivy. Now it's the talk of Uglytown! And you know what that means! Licensing!

Despite big-time success, Big Toe's place is still just like home. You can come back years later and still find the same wad of gum you left under the table as a child! Now that's what we call a real neighborhood classic.

Some of the Uglys feel like Big Toe's getting too corporate, but booby traps should take care of them.

Now if Big Toe could just get the food to look like it does in his TV ads!

WHAT'S ON THE
MENU?
Tastes Like It Looks
RefurBISHED Deluxe
5¢
Fried wedgeheads
5¢
Face on MARS cheese Block
30¢
ON
ROBOT ARM BENTO BOX
5¢
general-Age-guess muffin
50% off
Boiled Ice Cream
3¢
IMITATION UNICORN
10¢
STUPID MILK
5¢
STUPID MILK, FAMILY SIZE
80¢
ON SPECIAL
BOOM SHAKA LAKA
3¢
gingerBread MAN
2¢
EAT SLOW! we're TALKin' Three Fries MAX.
HOTLine 1-800-BUY
TALKing OX VALUE MeaL
99¢
NOT JUST A SALAD
20¢
PLASTIC PUPPET gLove
80¢
SPICY Ice
5¢
HOT Ice
8¢
BASKET of MYSTERY
5¢

Diet Special
TAKO CONE with cheese 20¢
Single Piece of cereal 80¢
Lukewarm Hot Dog WATER
ew!
House wine 20¢
Mwaha-haha.
Yes
no
Fortune 500 5¢
1+2+3+4 +5+600LBS 5¢
Play with your Food MASK 5¢
MAYOR B-GONE SPEECH Shortener 5¢
DuDe, we are TOAST!
what a JAM.
ugh...
BAD Joke meal 5¢
Never-FULL Coffee 2¢
Licensed uglyworm Juice 5¢
what DAT
SMALL PLASTIC TOY of the MASCOT 81¢
DRINKY SWORD CASE 10¢
ENCORE
Best Burger you ever had Back again 18¢
Fried ICE Barnacles 5¢
SIDE thingies with accessories 5¢
Hotcakes 5¢
DieT Hotcakes 5¢

MIND YOUR MANNERS! KNOW YOUR CHOW-DOWN ETIQUETTE

Table manners are very important. Like they always say, you have to learn the rules before you can break them. (Or something like that.)

DUDE, THAT'S **RUDE**.

Just follow these simple rules and the likelihood of others' running away from you will decrease dramatically.

Please mind your choice of words when asking the waiter to identify someone else's meal.

We do o
ASK ABOUT OUR
SPECIALS
ALL YOU want... we won't TALK. Never!
No, WAIT.
Time WAits for those who wait.
Hey... we're out of Food!

Banking.
UGLY DINER
Sorry! I got the MUNCHIES.
Is ANYone going to WAit on us?
I'm WAiting.

RESERVATIONS!
I have reservations ABOUT Making Reservations.
WHOA! I'm in A BUBBLE!
I can get in... NO proBLem.
go CHICAgo!
Don't forget to make reservations!
Just make a quick switcheroo.
you're always NEXT!
you
not you
not you
not you
not you
not you
not you
not you
not you
OX & WEDGEHEAD'S Reservation Book
SLOW night. OK, you're NEXT.
Sorry, I Don't see...
RAD!
AW, com on.
Chez Fancy Pants
PODIUM -O- RAMA
But in case you do,
Wedgehead and Ox's
Reservation-Podium-O-Rama
service works every time.
OX & WEDGEHEAD's Reservation Podium!
NOT EVERY ESTABLISHMENT TAKES RESERVATIONS!
This is A BAKERY!
TABLE FOR ONE!

If you do need to make reservations in Uglytown, be honest. Disguising your voice as some big-shot celebrity is not going to get you very far.

School lunch is the best . . . and sometimes the fastest way to the nurse's office! But really, it all depends on what you choose.

An apple a day keeps the doctor away, but Apple Pie with Tako Cone Cream on top keeps your doctor in his sports car with the heated seats. It's all up to you.

Watch out for bullies! If they get cramps from the lunch paid for with money stolen from you, you could be liable.

Restaurants aplenty in the Uglyverse.
So what are you in the mood for?
Spicy? Trendy? Fishy? Smelly?
If you don't have reservations, you will
once you're done . . . about many things!

BABO'Z
COOKIEZ
ZZZ
Put A Z on the end to make $
BABO'S COOKIE LOFT
COOKIEZ
YUMMYZ
TUMMY HURTZ!
TRENDY EATZ
"The USUAL"
SAME Cafe
wha DatZ!
BABO'S COOKIE LOFT
TRENDY!
SMALL
CREATURE OF HABIT
STILL OPEN

BABO'S COOKIE KITCHEN

Babo makes the best cookies in Uglytown. You can smell the cookies baking from miles away!

The line for his Chocolate Chip Monster Bite usually goes round the block.

Uglys have often wondered why each of Babo's cookies comes with what looks a lot like a bite already taken out of it. What a unique design concept!

But you'd better hurry.
Babo is his own best customer.

UH-OH! I'M FAT!

Eating out too often can sometimes result in weight gain.

And while being overweight means glamorous living and a movie-star lifestyle, the truth of the matter is that it's not very good for you!

With healthier food choices and lots of exercise, the glamour may fade but you will feel great and maybe even live a whole lot longer! (So long as you avoid falling into an open manhole, going to bad movies, story time with Chuckanucka, and stuff like that.)

Remember, it's not what the scale tells you so much as how your clothes fit you. Unless you're naked, like Wedgehead. Then go by the scale. Especially if it breaks.

PLUNKO'S

BUFFET LIKE NO OTHER

In the Uglyverse, life is a lot like a buffet. Don't worry about what everyone else is eating.

Don't ever worry about what the most popular dish is . . . even if you're the only one who likes what you like and others mock you. Anyway, blueberries with broccoli is a very healthy choice . . . gross or not.

Being the only one doesn't make you wrong. You may not even want to eat from the buffet. You might hold out for something better. Something different. Your snack is out there . . . you have to go find it. Others will try to talk you out of it. It's out there, though . . . with a cherry on top.

If a time traveler from the future told you that your lifelong dreams would not come true, would you still go for them? If your answer is yes, then you will succeed. Now get out there and show us what you got. The Uglys got your back.

These are the top-four most popular eateries at the moment. Let's see if your taste buds agree! Let's see if your wallet runs away. . . .

Trunko 2 Go will get you on your way in no time! That way they can get to the next guy even quicker . . . cha-ching!

At the Manboat Root Beer Float Moat, we highly recommend the special . . . next door at Moxy's BBQ.

At Moxy's BBQ, the only thing fried is your brain as you wrap your mind around their thought-provoking menu. Culinary arts minus the smarts!

Uglys LOVE the Interdimensional Coffeehouse of Cheese. You walk in today and come out yesterday. Something like that.

EATING ON THE PLANE

we missed our flight!

Awesome!

whew!

EEEWWWW!!

wedgehead Air

Eating on the plane is great! You have a microsecond to decide between chicken and beef, which is great for the vegetarians. But even better, you have to get it all down before the cleanup cart comes by, all while sitting in a space smaller than your body and making sure not to spill hot drinks on your neighbor during turbulence (which comes along only once everyone has been served).

Just kidding! Awesome idea for a sci-fi movie, right?

Ever fold your food tray in half only to find a shallow indentation some call a cup holder?

Well, in the Uglyverse they call it a hot-beverage balancing game.
Let's play freshly brewed coffee tightrope!
Here comes the air pocket!

SAY WHEN!

When is enough enough? How do we know when we've had more than we can handle? In the Uglyverse, you can have as much of something as you believe you can, but do you need it all? What do you really need? IS what you need and what you want one and the same? Yeah, baby! . . . CHOCOLATE!!!! Woohoo!